TURNING POINTS

THE REFUGEE CRISIS

BY MICHAEL E. GOODMAN

CREATIVE EDUCATION • CREATIVE PAPERBACKS

Published by Creative Education and Creative Paperbacks
P.O. Box 227, Mankato, Minnesota 56002
Creative Education and Creative Paperbacks are imprints of
The Creative Company
www.thecreativecompany.us

Design by The Design Lab
Production by Colin O'Dea
Art direction by Rita Marshall
Printed in China

Photographs by Alamy (Rehman Asad, Olivier Asselin, Dave Bagnall Collection, ITAR-TASS News Agency, PixelPro), Getty Images (AFP Contributor/ AFP, Barcroft Media, KENA BETANCUR/Stringer/AFP, Bettmann, Terry Fincher/ Stringer/Hulton Archive, Handout/Getty Images News, Chris Hondros/ Getty Images News, HERIKA MARTINEZ/AFP, Chris Minihane/Moment, Print Collector/Hulton Archive, Zacharie Rabehi/EyeEm, Michael Rougier/The LIFE Picture Collection, Srdjan Stevanovic/Stringer/Getty Images News, Universal History Archive/Universal Images Group), iStockphoto (brunoat, Joel Carillet, EdnaM, ranplett, sadikgulec, tatakis)

TABLE *of* CONTENTS

I n March 2011, many Arab countries in the Middle East and northern Africa were undergoing political unrest. Several leaders lost power, and new governments were established. This period of unrest became known as the "Arab Spring." In the midst of the Arab Spring, a group of children in Daraa, a city in southwestern Syria, decided to make a political statement of their own. They painted a message in Arabic on a wall. It read: "Down with the system." Syria's president, Bashar al-Assad, reacted strongly to what he saw as an act of rebellion. The children were arrested and tortured. When adults in Daraa marched and demanded the children be released, Assad's forces fired into the protesters, killing three people. Those were the first shots fired in a **civil war** that quickly engulfed Syria.

Makeshift structures meant to provide temporary shelter for refugees may often become home for years while displaced people remain in limbo.

War raged in Syria for the next seven years. Many Syrians joined or supported the rebel forces against Assad's government; others backed Assad. Rebel forces tried to gain footholds in different parts of the country but were violently turned back by pro-Assad forces. More than 400,000 people—both soldiers and **civilians**—were killed as the two sides battled. Bombs, missiles, and fires also demolished hundreds of thousands of buildings and destroyed farming areas. As a result, millions of Syrian civilians found themselves homeless, jobless, hungry, and on the move. They streamed like a human river toward bordering countries, desperately searching for a safe place to live and raise their families. What began in Syria as a political struggle had evolved into the world's latest refugee crisis.

In 19th-century New York City, Italian immigrants converged on Manhattan's Mulberry Street, and the area became the heart of "Little Italy."

CHAPTER ONE

FLEEING FROM PERIL

Throughout history, people have been on the move. Sometimes they moved to flee life-threatening **famines** or natural disasters, such as floods, **tsunamis**, or volcanic eruptions. Sometimes they moved to escape persecution because of their religious or political beliefs. Sometimes they moved to avoid the dangers and destruction of war. Most often they moved in hopes of finding a better opportunity for their family in a new place.

People who move to a new place are called *migrants*. In the 1680s, a special word was coined to describe migrants who were forced to leave their home country because their lives were threatened—*refugees*. The new word was based on the French word *refuge*, which means "a hiding place." The first people actually called refugees were groups of French Protestants,

Pocket watch

known as Huguenots. Because most French people in the 1600s were Roman Catholics, the Huguenots often faced **religious discrimination**. In 1685, Louis XIV enacted a law that forced Huguenots to give up their religion

Jews from Russian lands entered the United States in massive numbers during the 1890s: more than 100,000 came in 1891 and 1892 respectively.

and become Catholics or face prison or death. More than 200,000 Huguenots chose to leave France instead. Many of these refugees went to other countries in Europe, such as England or the Netherlands. Some sailed across the Atlantic Ocean to the American colonies and settled primarily in parts of New York and New Jersey.

Religious discrimination, famine, and war drove large numbers of Europeans to become refugees in the 19th and early 20th centuries. In the 1840s and 1850s, a terrible fungus destroyed the potato crops on which Irish farmers and

POINTING OUT

WELCOME AND UNWELCOME

*The Huguenots were generally well received in America. Another early group of refugees was not as welcome. In the early 1800s, black slaves rebelled against white landowners in what is now Haiti, demanding an end to slavery. The violence and destruction led thousands of both white Haitians and freed blacks to seek **asylum** in the new United States. The refugees received a mixed welcome. Whites were generally accepted, while some blacks were viewed as potential troublemakers. The influx of Haitian refugees had a major impact on several U.S. cities. For example, when 10,000 Haitian refugees began arriving in New Orleans in 1810, they doubled the city's population.*

peasants depended. Residents said they could smell decaying plants and even dead bodies in many Irish farming areas. According to one farmer, "I saw the crop, I smelt the fearful stench, now so well-known and recognized as the death-sign of each field of potatoes." In all, more than a million people died during the potato famine, and nearly twice that many Irish people sailed to North America or Australia as refugees.

Starting in the 1880s, more than 2 million Jewish refugees left lands ruled by Russia—including Poland, Latvia, Lithuania, and the Ukraine—seeking safety and religious freedom. Most came to North America. They were fleeing deadly and destructive attacks called pogroms in which many Jewish homes and synagogues were burned, and thousands of people were killed. Many young Jewish men also left to avoid being forced to join the Russian army, where they were often treated badly. One leader in the Ukraine wrote about the need for Jews to migrate: "There is no hope for [Jews] in Russia, our birthplace. . . . In America we shall find rest; the stars and stripes will wave over the true home of our people. To America, brethren! To America!"

Terrible poverty and famine in southern Italy also drove millions of Italian families to leave their country and sail across the Atlantic. More than 3 million Italians immigrated to America between 1900 and 1915. All of these groups had a

common connection: They had left their native homelands permanently, believing they could never return because of the threats of starvation or persecution.

Up until the late 1800s, there were few laws limiting the ability of people to move from one country to another. Moving mainly required courage and enough money to pay for transportation. In addition, most governments willingly accepted healthy immigrants. However, after World War I began in 1914, many countries tightened their borders and created special travel documents called passports or visas to regulate immigration. Some countries also passed laws to keep out foreigners, fearing they might bring crime or unwelcome political views with them. These new laws and regulations made it harder for people made homeless during or after the war to find new places to live.

Social scientists classified these homeless people into two categories. Those who crossed an international border and left their country permanently because of war or persecution were defined as *refugees*. Those who became homeless but stayed in the same country were defined as *internally displaced persons*. Historians estimate that a combined 10 million people in both categories were driven from their homes during World War I or during the political upheavals that followed in countries such as Russia, Turkey,

POINTING OUT

A SOLITARY REFUGEE

For nearly 20 years, Mehran Karimi Nasseri's only legal home was a terminal in Charles de Gaulle Airport in Paris. A native of Iran, Nasseri was expelled for protesting, and his passport was taken away. He was finally granted a Belgian passport—but then that was stolen. Even without a passport, he boarded a plane in Paris to fly to England, where he was turned away and flown back to Paris. French officials arrested Nasseri but could not send him back to Iran, nor would Belgian officials allow him back. Instead, he lived as a celebrity in the Paris airport for 18 years. His story was the inspiration for the 2004 movie The Terminal.

and Spain. Fortunately, most were able either to return home or to resettle in new lands within a few years.

However, even greater refugee crises lay ahead. During World War II (1939–45), foreign armies occupied territory or fought battles on many different fronts—Europe, North Africa, the Far East, and the Pacific. Death and destruction took place everywhere. When the war ended, 60 million Europeans and tens of millions of Chinese and other Asian peoples were left homeless. What could be done to find suitable homes for all these people and to help

them rebuild their lives?

One possible answer involved a new international body known as the United Nations (UN). The UN was formed in 1945 as a place where the leaders of different nations could meet and try to settle differences without going to war. The UN was also intended to be a resource for solving international problems, such as what to do with refugees. Starting in July 1947, a UN-sponsored agency known as the International Relief Organization (IRO) began assisting refugees and displaced persons in many European and Asian countries. The IRO established displaced person (DP) camps to shelter and care for many people left homeless by the war. It also helped those in the camps reunite with relatives from whom they had been separated.

In 1951, a new UN agency, the UN High Commissioner for Refugees (UNHCR), was created to take over and expand the work of the IRO. The UNHCR's early tasks included defining exactly who a refugee is and setting forth rules and procedures to protect refugees' rights. One important but controversial rule was that once a person who met the definition of *refugee* crossed into another country and requested asylum, the second country must evaluate the request and determine if asylum should be granted.

The UNHCR developed a recordkeeping system for registering refugees and monitoring their movements. It also worked out cooperative agreements with aid organizations and charitable groups such as Save the Children, Doctors Without Borders, and the International Rescue Committee to help care for refugee families in camps. In the 70 years since its founding, the UNHCR has expanded its geographical scope to deal with refugee crises all around the world. When the Syrian Civil War broke out in 2011, it presented the UNHCR with one of its greatest challenges yet. Soon more than half of that country's population was on the move. The human movement of Syrian refugees has greatly affected life in many other countries as well.

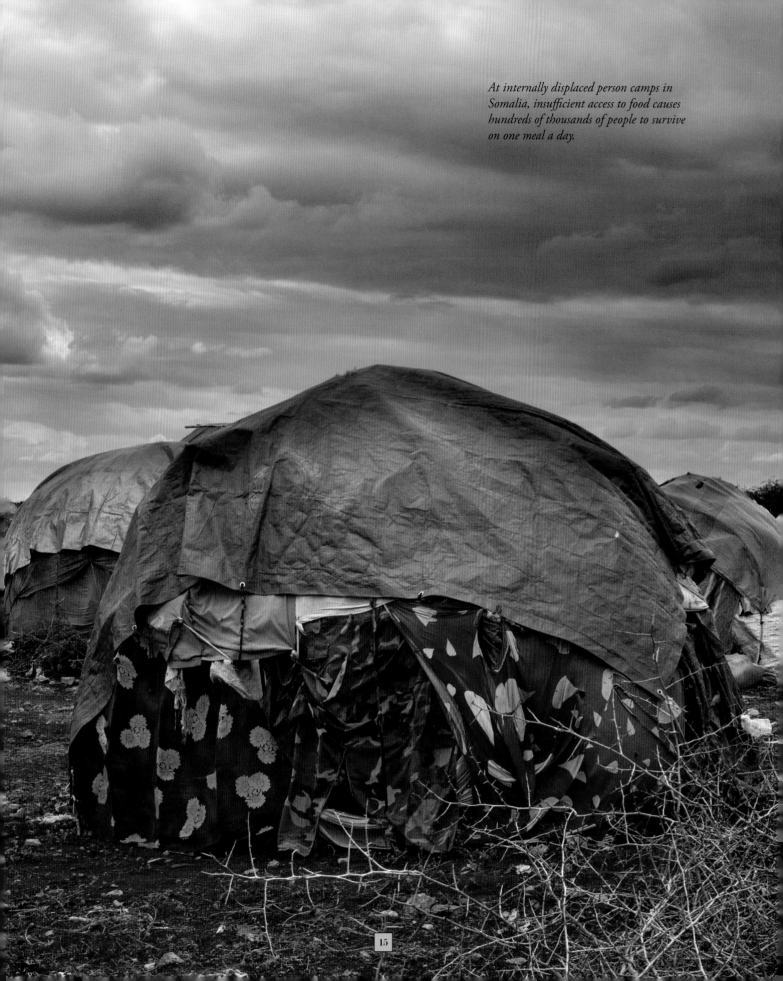

At internally displaced person camps in Somalia, insufficient access to food causes hundreds of thousands of people to survive on one meal a day.

CHAPTER TWO

GOING GLOBAL

The end of World War II marked a turning point in the global refugee crisis. At first, UN agencies focused primarily on the rescue and resettlement of European nationals still displaced after the war ended. But refugee problems were not limited to Europe. Over the next 70 years, the series of dramatic events and violent conflicts described in the following pages displaced people all around the globe. In response, the UNHCR expanded its efforts to monitor and assist refugees in Asia, Africa, the Middle East, and Central America as well.

In 1948, the state of Israel was formally established as a homeland for Jews. Almost immediately, 700,000 **Muslim** Palestinians chose to or were forced to leave towns and villages that were now legally part of Israel. Relations between Israelis and Palestinians are still tense, and there is a charged atmosphere throughout the Middle East surrounding the plight of Palestinian refugees. The UN Relief and Welfare Agency (UNRWA) has primary responsibility for this crisis area and currently serves more than 5 million Palestinian refugees in camps and facilities located throughout the region.

Between 1945 and 1953, a conflict raged between **communist** North Korea and democratic South Korea. The two countries had formerly been united, but their political differences forced them apart. It was more than a civil

Children and families in African countries become refugees not only because of political instability but also from extreme weather events such as droughts.

Heavy street fighting caused many Vietnamese to flee their villages and cities; they returned only once hostilities had abated.

war. Many other countries, such as China, the Soviet Union, and the United States, took sides and sent in troops and weapons. During the Korean War, as many as 900,000 North Koreans crossed into South Korea. Millions more Koreans on both sides were displaced by the violence and destruction.

Also during that time, the Soviet Union brought many Eastern European countries under its influence. It appointed leaders for these countries and forced them to adopt strict laws that limited personal independence of their residents. Many people objected to the new national laws and to the communist philosophy of the Soviet Union. Hundreds of thousands of Eastern Europeans fled to Western Europe or North America. Other unhappy citizens stayed behind and took part in revolutions against their governments.

Hungarian revolutionary

In 1956, thousands of students in Hungary staged a protest against Soviet rule of their country. The Soviet Union sent in soldiers and tanks and violently ended the revolt. More than 250,000 Hungarians left the country as refugees. Another anti-Soviet revolt took place in Czechoslovakia in 1968. It, too, was put down quickly, but nearly 50,000 Czechs also became refugees.

A civil war in Vietnam escalated into a major international conflict in the late 1960s. More than 2.7 million Americans fought alongside South Vietnamese soldiers in the war against soldiers from communist North Vietnam and its allies, especially China and the Soviet Union. By the time the costly and deadly war ended in 1975, nearly 3 million people had become homeless. Approximately 1.6 million Vietnamese chose to flee. Many refugees feared for their lives because they had fought with or worked for the Americans during the war. Most tried to escape by boat. At the direction of president Gerald Ford, the U.S. government organized airlifts to bring 100,000 Vietnamese refugees to America. Ford explained, "To ignore the refugees in their hour of need would be to repudiate the values we cherish as a nation of immigrants."

Wars in Afghanistan and the **Balkans** in the 1990s and in Iraq starting in 2003 brought more destruction and displaced more people who required assistance from the UNHCR. Around the same time, the UN was also drawn into a new

POINTING OUT

A SPECIAL SWIMMER

In 2011, 13-year-old Yusra Mardini was training to become an Olympic swimmer for Syria. Then war broke out in her country. She and her sister Sarah, also a swimmer, fled to Turkey in 2015. They paid **human smugglers** *to help them sail from Turkey to Greece as a first step toward gaining asylum in Germany. However, their boat over-turned in Greek waters. Yusra and Sarah jumped into the sea and helped guide the boat and its passengers to safety. In August 2016, Yusra made another important swim. She raced across a pool at the Olympic Games in Rio de Janeiro as a member of a special team composed of refugee athletes.*

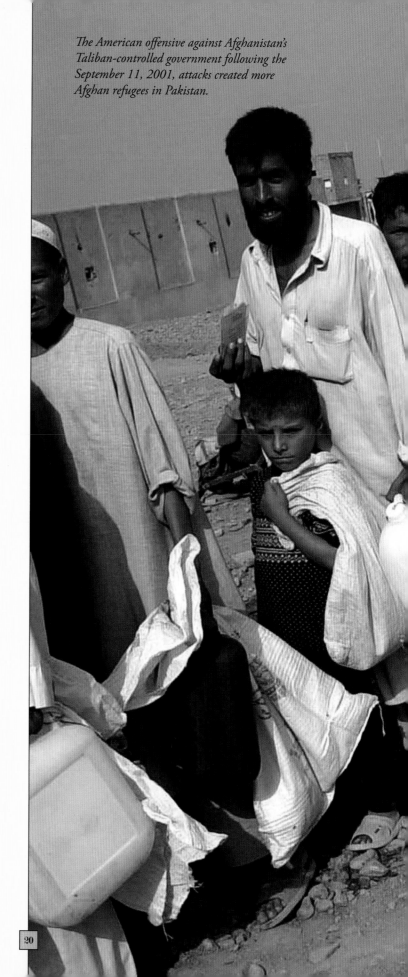

The American offensive against Afghanistan's Taliban-controlled government following the September 11, 2001, attacks created more Afghan refugees in Pakistan.

area of the world—Africa. A civil war between the northern and southern regions of Sudan started in 1983 and raged for more than 20 years. It disrupted the lives of millions of people and led to mass migrations from one of the poorest areas in the world. In the western region of Sudan known as Darfur, more than 3,300 villages were destroyed in conflicts between different tribal groups in 2003. Violence broke out again in Sudan in 2013, leading to another refugee flow.

In the midst of the Sudanese conflicts, tribal warfare that began in 1994 in the central African nation of Rwanda introduced a new term into the refugee crisis vocabulary: "ethnic cleansing." Ethnic cleansing is the mass expulsion or killing of

Rohingya refugees in Bangladesh may be moved to an island in the Bay of Bengal, where the government is building structures to house 100,000.

a particular ethnic or religious group in an area by another group. In the Rwandan conflict, more than 500,000 members of the Tutsi tribe were killed by members of the Hutu tribe. More than 2 million Rwandans of both tribes fled from their homeland. Most were forced to move into DP camps in neighboring nations such as Zaire, Uganda, and Burundi.

The Syrian Civil War that began in 2011 quickly developed into the most devastating refugee crisis of them all. Syria had a population of 24 million before the war. Eight years later, nearly 5 million Syrians were living in other countries, and nearly 9 million were classified as internally displaced persons. The international community was faced with the question of how to respond to the needs of Syrian refugees. Neighboring countries such as Turkey, Jordan, and Lebanon took in the majority. Germany and Sweden were also very welcoming. Other countries such as Hungary, Austria, and the U.S. were not as generous.

As of 2018, the fastest-growing refugee crisis in the world was taking place among the Rohingya people of Myanmar, a nation in Southeast Asia. The Rohingya are a Muslim minority in a country that is predominantly Buddhist. They have their own language and culture. In recent years, the government refused to recognize the Rohingya as citizens. Many of their villages were burned down by government troops and local Buddhist mobs.

Nearly one million Rohingya chose to flee. Most went to neighboring Bangladesh, where they moved into quickly constructed **refugee camps** or into towns. Because Bangladesh is a very poor country, it has had difficulty accommodating the influx.

Responding to the needs of refugees has become a global concern. It is a political problem because it involves decisions that governments must make about whether to allow migrating homeless people to cross their borders. It is a **humanitarian** problem because it involves finding ways to care for people—particularly children—who cannot be independently responsible for their own housing, food, education, and health needs. It is an economic problem because many of the world's poorest nations are being called upon to bear much of the cost of caring for refugees who have crossed their borders.

CHAPTER THREE

REFUGEE LIFE

Just how widespread a problem is today's global refugee crisis? Statistics compiled by the UNHCR indicate that, as of the end of 2017, there were 68.5 million people who had been forced to leave their homes because of political or religious persecution, war, or conflict between ethnic groups. The total included 25.4 million refugees and 40 million internally displaced persons—or 1 out of every 110 people living in the world. Nearly half were under the age of 18.

Another 3.1 million refugees fell into a third category—those seeking asylum. Asylum seekers are individuals who flee to another country and ask that new country to allow them to stay legally. So, asylum seekers are legally "between" countries. They are permanently giving up their rights in one country and asking for protection inside another one. To be granted asylum, individuals must demonstrate that they have a legitimate fear that returning to their old homes would be life-threatening and not just an economic hardship. In granting asylum, the new country agrees to provide

UNHCR refugee tents

In Algeria, middle-aged inhabitants of Sahrawi refugee camps
have never known a permanent
home—their people have been
refugees for 50 years.

More than 650 miles' (1,046 km) worth of fencing demarcated portions of the U.S. border with Mexico as of early 2019.

the asylum seeker with certain legal rights and protection. In most cases, the new country also agrees to provide asylum seekers with temporary financial and employment assistance until they can fully care for themselves.

In recent years, the U.S. has become an important destination for asylum seekers from Latin America. Most seeking asylum in the U.S. are trying to escape the violence and crime of Central America's Northern Triangle—the region encompassing Guatemala, Honduras, and El Salvador. The process of being granted asylum in the U.S. can take several years. Many Latin

POINTING OUT

BOAT PEOPLE

The fall of South Vietnam to North Vietnam in 1975 spurred many Vietnamese, Cambodians, and Laotians to become refugees and escape the communist takeover of their countries. More than 800,000 people fled on boats of all sizes. Many boats were not seaworthy. Others were dangerously overcrowded. The "boat people" braved storms and pirate attacks as well as starvation and disease. Between 200,000 and 400,000 died at sea. Most who survived relocated at first to refugee camps in other Southeast Asian countries. Some stayed in those countries permanently. Others sought asylum in other countries, including the U.S., Canada, and Australia.

Even before Trump took office as the 45th president, those who disagreed with his policies and attitudes took to protesting in public.

American refugees, unwilling or unable to wait for legal admission into the U.S., have attempted to cross the American border illegally.

Arguments about policing illegal immigration or granting asylum have become heated among American politicians and citizens. The arguments reached crisis level in 2018 when American president Donald Trump's administration attempted to shut down the country's southern border with Mexico to most refugees and to significantly reduce the number of asylum requests it would process. Many families trying to come across the border were stopped, and, in some cases, children were separated from their parents as a way to deter refugees from attempting border crossings in the future.

Even though the U.S. and some other countries have put up more barriers to refugees, intense fear and distress still drive millions to cross national borders. Most hope their stay outside their home country will be a short one and that they will be able to return home when conditions change. Others hope that they will be granted asylum in the new country and can eventually become citizens, creating successful lives for themselves and their families. But their hopes don't always become reality.

For most refugees, the decision to leave their country is a desperate one. Their lives are on the line, and they do not have time for careful planning. They have to move quickly, and their trip is often very dangerous. Many refugees are young children or teenagers. Some travel with their parents or other family members. Some are alone, often pushed to flee by their parents who must stay behind to take care of older relatives or other family members.

Many refugees escape on foot, often walking hundreds of miles through dangerous, war-torn areas or over difficult terrain. Others make their way using whatever means of transportation is possible to get to another country where they feel they will be safe. Sometimes this trip involves paying money to a human smuggler who agrees to move them across a border. Many smugglers are dishonest, however. They take the refugees' money and then abandon them before or during the trip. Or the smugglers may pack their human cargo onto overcrowded trucks or in unsafe boats, running the risk of killing many of the passengers.

Once refugees cross a border into a neighboring country, most have no specific destination in mind, such as a relative's home. They simply need to find shelter and food quickly. For many travelers, their first stop is a refugee camp, and their first shelter is often one of hundreds of tents or other simple structures put up in a flat area near the border of their old country. The camp is usually overcrowded, with insufficient food, water, and medical supplies for all the

inhabitants and primitive toilet facilities. The camp has been designed to be a temporary home for refugees, but many will stay in the camp for years or even decades.

Some refugee camps are truly like cities. The world's largest refugee camp is Kutupalong in Bangladesh. It is the temporary home for more than 800,000 Rohingya who have fled from religious persecution in Myanmar. Two camps in Kenya, Dadaab and Kakuma, house more than 400,000 refugees fleeing violence in Sudan, Somalia, and Ethiopia.

POINTING OUT

WORLD REFUGEE DAY

Since 2000, the UN has designated June 20 as World Refugee Day. According to the UN's website, "On World Refugee Day … we commemorate the strength, courage, and perseverance of millions of refugees. World Refugee Day also marks a key moment for the public to show support for families forced to flee." Many churches and religious groups publish World Refugee Day Toolkits with activities for serving and honoring refugees. HIAS, a Jewish organization that serves immigrants and refugees, has designated a special Sabbath for honoring refugees around the world. The first Refugee Shabbat was held on October 18, 2018.

The sprawling Za'atari camp is organized into 12 districts, and aid organizations such as Oxfam are working to improve sanitation and water supplies.

Half of the population of Za'atari is under the age of 18—younger than this young man, Musa Mahameed, age 19, who planned to return to Syria.

Za'atari, which is located in Jordan, just across the Syrian border, is the largest camp in the Middle East. It is home to 85,000 Syrian refugees. That makes it Jordan's fourth-largest city. Most of the homes are large **prefabricated** boxes with electrical connections but no running water or plumbing facilities. These facilities are provided in communal locations. Some skilled residents have found ways to weld together several boxes to accommodate their larger families.

The homes have been laid out in patterns with unpaved paths between them to allow ambulances, water trucks, or other vehicles to pass. Many ambitious refugees have set up businesses on streets in Za'atari, such as bakeries, barbershops, cafes, and even a pet shop and a pizza delivery service. The largest business street in the camp has been jokingly named the Champs Elysees, after the fanciest street in Paris, France.

Camps are vital for many refugees. However, UNHCR statistics indicate that two-thirds of refugees do not stay in camps. Instead, most move to or hide in a city or town in the new country. Life is often difficult for refugees in these urban settings. Finding their own housing and food can be problematic and expensive. There are also few government services provided for these "foreigners." In many cases, local laws or regulations also do not permit noncitizens to work and earn money. In some ways, refugees are as isolated in cities as they would be in camps.

REFUGEE STORIES

D avid Miliband, president of the International Rescue Committee, is one of the world's leading experts on refugee rights and management. In his book *Rescue: Refugees and the Political Crisis of Our Time*, Miliband writes: "If you look at the statistics [about the global refugee problem], you get depressed. If you look at the people, you find hope." Here are hopeful stories about three young refugees:

Salva Dut was born in the southern part of Sudan in 1974. When he was a child, a civil war broke out between the Muslim leaders in the north—who ran the national government and wanted all Sudanese to be Muslims—and the Dinka and Nuer tribes who lived in the south. Salva was Dinka. At age 11, his village was attacked, and he joined 17,000 other Sudanese boys on a long journey to safety across the border into Ethiopia. These boys became known as the "Lost Boys from Sudan." Salva stayed in a refugee camp in Ethiopia for five years until a war broke out in that country. Then he led more than 1,500 boys on a perilous walk for hundreds of miles through the Sudanese desert to the UN-run Kakuma refugee camp in Kenya, where he stayed for six years.

In 1996, Salva was one of 3,000 "lost boys" invited to live in the U.S. He was welcomed by a family in Rochester, New York. Salva went to school

Refugees and migrants who venture into cities may end up taking shelter in abandoned buildings that do not have proper heating.

At a camp in Uganda, South Sudanese refugees wait to be resettled after fleeing violence and destruction at home.

in Rochester and then enrolled in a local college to study business. In January 2002, Salva learned from a fellow refugee that his father was seriously ill. He traveled back home for the first time in 16 years. There he found out that the biggest problem facing most people in his country was the availability of clean water. Salva returned to Rochester and formed a new company called Water for South Sudan (WFSS). The company raised money to drill wells to supply water for the South Sudanese people. Salva personally took charge of drilling the first WFSS well in his father's village in 2005. Since that time, WFSS has

POINTING OUT

FROM SUDAN TO THE NBA

When Minnesota Timberwolves basketball star Luol Deng was four, his family fled from South Sudan to Egypt. It was not a happy time. "I remember when I was a kid as a refugee in Egypt, every day there was always a hope that we would get to leave tomorrow, that we would go where we would have more opportunity." Deng's family moved to England when he was 10, and by age 13, he was already one of that country's best basketball players. He came to the U.S. to play for high school and college teams. In 2004, Deng was the seventh overall draft pick in the National Basketball Association (NBA).

drilled nearly 300 wells in South Sudan, producing clean water for more than a quarter of a million people every day. Today, Salva lives in South Sudan and runs his company there.

Growing up in a rocky part of Afghanistan, Shukria Rezaei loved going to school, but it wasn't easy to do. "School was two mountains away, and it snowed a lot," she recalled. "We went on a rocky mountain path and it took an hour and a half." One subject she studied was English. She also read and recited a lot of poetry in her native language. She never realized that both of those subjects would be important to her life.

Before she was 10, Shukria's family fled to Pakistan to escape fighting in Afghanistan. Her father applied for asylum in the United Kingdom. Three years later, he was able to bring Shukria and her mother to Oxford, England. At school in Oxford, Shukria struggled at first until her English improved. She was also shy and didn't stand out in school. Then she began writing her own poetry in English. Her teachers and classmates were impressed, and Shukria was judged to be the best poet in her grade. She won the poetry prize in school, and then she earned a scholarship to the University of London. She has continued to write poetry, and her work has been published in several well-respected British magazines. The following is an excerpt from one of Shukria's poems. It shows her feelings about her refugee experience:

A Glass of Tea (after Rumi)

Last year, I held a glass of tea to the light. This year,
I swirl like a tealeaf in the streets of Oxford.
Last year, I stared into navy blue sky. This year,
I am roaming under colourless clouds.
Last year, I watched the dazzling sun dance gracefully. This year,
The faint sun moves futurelessly.
Migration drove me down this bumpy road,
Where I fell and smelt the soil, where I arose and sensed the cloud.

José Garcia's family did not like living in Cuba under the harsh rule of communist **dictator** Fidel Castro. For many years, they hoped to escape to the U.S. America was only 90 miles (145 km), but it seemed to be a world away. Then in April 1980, Castro announced that for the next seven months, any Cubans who wished to leave Cuba for the U.S. would be allowed to board boats at the port of Mariel, west of Havana, as long as they had someone to meet them in the U.S. Thirteen-year-old José and his parents paid a $1,000-per-passenger fee for passage on a small boat, excited to finally make a journey to freedom. However, the boat didn't go anywhere for several days. Storms

Despite ongoing conflict in Syria, it remains a place of refuge to more than 400,000 Palestinians living in 12 camps there.

made the waters of the Caribbean Sea unsafe to sail on, but guards in the port would not let any passengers leave their boats. Soon, food supplies were running low, and many passengers became sick.

José's boat was finally permitted to sail, but its engines died within an hour from shore. High waves washed over the boat's deck, and everyone aboard thought they were going to drown. Luckily, a shrimp boat pulled up and allowed the passengers from José's boat to pile aboard. The now-overcrowded shrimp boat was also soon hit by a storm and was on the verge of capsizing. José was not a religious person, but he started to pray. Luckily, his prayers were answered when the U.S.

POINTING OUT

EMMA'S TORCH

An unusual restaurant in Brooklyn, New York, serves as a training ground for refugees learning to cook foods from their native countries. Emma's Torch is named for the poet Emma Lazarus, who wrote the poem inscribed on the base of the Statue of Liberty, which includes the words "Give me your tired, your poor, your huddled masses yearning to breathe free." The restaurant sponsors a graduation dinner each month where diners can sample foods prepared by trainees. At one such dinner, the menu included foods from Ethiopia, Vietnam, Turkey, and Jamaica.

As part of the Mariel Boatlift in 1980, 125,000 Cubans packed onto only about 1,700 boats to flee to Florida.

Coast Guard arrived and towed the boat to Key West, Florida. The 7-hour trip had taken more than 18 hours. After a short time in Florida, José's family settled in New York, and then they moved to New Jersey, where he went to high school and then to college.

Today, José is a professor at Florida Southern College. In 2010, he made a documentary film called *Voices from Mariel* about the experience of Cuban refugees who took part in the Mariel Boatlift. In it, José described the prejudice that Cuban refugees faced both in the U.S. and in Cuba. Castro labeled the refugees *scoria*, a Spanish word meaning "trash." He said he was happy that the trash had left Cuba. José was just as happy to be as far away from Castro as he could get.

Every refugee has a different story to tell. Most of their stories involve life-threatening situations, hard journeys, and difficult adjustments to new ways of life. But the journeys must be made in order to stay alive. Poet Warsan Shire, whose parents were Somali refugees, described why refugees take the risks that they do: "No one puts their children in a boat unless the water is safer than the land."

1685	French king Louis XIV revokes the Edict of Nantes, forbidding French Huguenots from practicing their religion.
1881	Russian czar Alexander II's assassination sets off anti-Jewish riots. Two million Jewish refugees come to the U.S.
1918	World War I ends. More than 10 million people are displaced.
1945	World War II ends, leaving as many as 60 million people displaced. The UN is established as a forum for bringing nations together.
1948	Israel is granted statehood by the UN. More than 700,000 Palestinians leave their homes.
1951	The UN High Commissioner for Refugees (UNHCR) is created. It helps define exactly who a refugee is and sets forth rules and procedures to protect refugees' rights.
1956	Hungarian students protest Soviet repression in their country. More than 200,000 refugees flee the country.
1975	North Vietnamese troops enter Saigon, the capital of South Vietnam, ending the war there. More than 800,000 "boat people" flee.
1979	Troops from the Soviet Union invade Afghanistan, and 5 million Afghanis flee.
1980	During the Mariel Boatlift, 125,000 Cubans leave their country and sail to the U.S.
1983–2005	A civil war in Sudan displaces nearly 4 million people.
1992–95	A civil war in the Balkans causes 2 million people to become refugees or internally displaced persons.
1994	A campaign of ethnic cleansing takes place in Rwanda. More than 500,000 Tutsi tribal members are killed by rival Hutus.
2003	Troops from the U.S. and several of its allies invade Iraq, toppling its leader, Saddam Hussein, and setting off a civil war.
2011–	Civil war breaks out in Syria. More than half the country's population is forced to leave their homes.
2017–	More than one million Rohingya Muslims begin leaving Myanmar because of religious persecution. Most flee to neighboring Bangladesh.

asylum—protection given by a government to individuals who have left another country because of fear for their lives

Balkans—a geographic area in southeastern Europe that used to be occupied by Yugoslavia but now includes the countries of Slovenia, Croatia, Bosnia and Herzegovina, Serbia, and Macedonia

civil war—a war between opposing groups of citizens of the same country

civilian—someone who is not a member of the military

communist—involving a system of government in which all property and business is owned and controlled by the state, with the goal of creating a classless society

dictator—a ruler with complete power, who often rules by force

famines—times of extreme scarcity of food, often caused by long periods of high temperatures and lack of rain

humanitarian—promoting ideas that improve the lives of people

human smugglers—individuals who take money to transport refugees across country borders by land, sea, or air; some smugglers are dishonest and endanger the lives of refugees

Muslim—a follower of Islam, a religion that says there is one God—Allah—and that Muhammad is his prophet

prefabricated—related to a structure that is manufactured in sections so it can be easily assembled

refugee camps—temporary places for refugees to live until they can find a permanent home; camps are usually set up by the United Nations, national governments, or non-governmental organizations, such as charities

religious discrimination—bad treatment given to individuals or groups because of their religious affiliation

social scientists—experts who study and write about how people live and relate to each other in areas such as economics, history, and politics

tsunamis—high, powerful sea waves, often caused by earthquakes, that can cause great damage and drown many people when they come ashore

Abouzeid, Rania. *No Turning Back: Life, Loss, and Hope in Wartime Syria.* New York: W. W. Norton, 2018.

Betts, Alexander, and Paul Collier. *Refuge: Rethinking Refugee Policy in a Changing World.* New York: Oxford University Press, 2017.

Dalton, David. *Living in a Refugee Camp: Carlito's Story.* Milwaukee, Wisc.: World Almanac Library, 2006.

Leatherdale, Mary Beth, and Eleanor Shakespeare. *Stormy Seas: Stories of Young Boat Refugees.* Toronto: Annick Press, 2017.

Marlowe, Jen, Aisha Bain, and Adam Shapiro. *Darfur Diaries: Stories of Survival.* New York: Nation Books, 2006.

Miliband, David. *Rescue: Refugees and the Political Crisis of Our Time.* New York: Simon & Schuster, 2017.

Park, Linda Sue. *A Long Walk to Water.* New York: Houghton Mifflin Harcourt, 2010.

Rawlence, Ben. *City of Thorns: Nine Lives in the World's Largest Refugee Camp.* New York: Picador, 2016.

Mercy Corps: Spend a Day with Nour
https://www.mercycorps.org/photoessays/jordan-syria/life-refugee-spend-day-nour
Learn about a Syrian teenager in Jordan's Za'atari refugee camp, and find
links to useful refugee-related topics.

United Nations High Commissioner for Refugees
http://www.unhcr.org/
Read about the activities of the UN organization that oversees refugee assistance around the world.

Note: Every effort has been made to ensure that the websites listed above are suitable for
children, that they have educational value, and that they contain no inappropriate material.
However, because of the nature of the Internet, it is impossible to guarantee that these sites
will remain active indefinitely or that their contents will not be altered.